# The House in the Middle of the Street

# The House in the Middle of the Street

Jennifer Sklias-Gahan

FOREWORD BY MARILYN MINTER

RARE BIRD

RARE BIRD • DEMIVOULA STUDIOS

6044 North Figueroa Street
Los Angeles, California 90042
rarebirdbooks.com



FIRST TRADE HARDCOVER EDITION



For more information, address:
Rare Bird Books Subsidiary Rights Department
6044 North Figueroa Street
Los Angeles, California 90042

*Illustrations by Myles Mullen*
Set in Dante

Printed in the United States

ISBN-13: 9781644285435

10 9 8 7 6 5 4 3 2 1

Library of Congress Cataloging-in-Publication Data
available upon request

# Contents

# A Word from the Author

Welcome to *The House in the Middle of the Street*. This house exists timelessly in the shadows of our family secrets, and its rules imposed on each who claim ownership of it. Set foot within its walls, where beautiful promises are made, heart-filled hopes are heard throughout the night, and our ravenous desires are revealed. All on the eve of a brand New Year.

As you enter, keep eyes wide open and attentive your ears. Perhaps, if you have a GOD, bring them with you. Kindly know, in life there are specific times and specific places, where instructions need to be followed. And though we are all fellow travelers, moving side by side, it is best to remember who and what we may be traveling with.

Before I go, do consider this: on certain days and on certain nights, if and when you hear a sturdy knocking at your front door, please, dear readers, please, be selective whom you invite in.

—JSG

# Foreword

by Marilyn Minter

Anyone who loves fairy tales will love this story. I couldn't get enough of them as a kid. The magic. And more so, the darkness. Because in the darkness is where every fairy tale unfolded. The good ones, anyway. So, when I read *The House in the Middle of the Street*, a story written by my friend of over twenty years, Jennifer Sklias-Gahan, I was immediately taken back. Because she created her own fairy tale.

A tale in which through the seemingly simple act of opening a door and inviting someone in, the reader is summoned to see the darker side of human nature, dependency, and insatiable desire. This isn't a happily ever after sort of tale for kids. It's a cautionary one for adults. One that channels life experience, real generational "curses" and the gaping holes of addiction. And that drives home the message that no matter how much we feed ourselves, we can still be empty. As an artist who explores similar subjects in visuals, I am enthralled by how Jennifer brought these themes to life through an almost rhythmic cadence. How she vividly describes her family of characters and the chilling atmosphere that surrounds them. The rest is for you as the reader to uncover. To reveal what layers of this story speak to you and your own history. But as you read, just remember this: on certain winter nights when your door is knocked upon—be selective just who you let in.

Marilyn Minter is an American artist currently living and working in New York City. Minter's work has been included in the Whitney Biennial, and installed several billboards in Chelsea, New York City in collaboration with Creative Time. Her video Green Pink Caviar was exhibited in the lobby of the MoMA from 2010–2011. Minter is represented by Salon 94, New York, Regen Projects, Los Angeles and Baldwin Gallery, Aspen.

# The House

There once was a house and it sat in the middle of a simple and quaint treelined street. A well worn grey stone wall lined its front yard. At its center stood a small wooden entry gate painted a clean white. The gate was marked with shiny black metal numbers that read seventeen. They glistened and matched its black handle which unlocked and opened easily with a light turn, leading you down a grey stone path to the front door. A beautiful woman named Rebecca lived in this house with her faithfully devoted husband. They were happy and they were proud.

The house had originally belonged to a Great Great Aunt of Rebecca's named Minerva. Minerva lived in the house all the days of her life and she died there, on the very last night of the year. She was found, on the morning of the New Year, dead in her house by Nester and his wife Agatha the house's long-time caretakers. They found her peacefully sleeping in her armchair. Beside Minerva on her table stood a simple glass jar, sealed with a shiny golden lid. The jar was marked with the date of the year just passed. Resting by the jar was a golden sealed envelope embossed with the initials MA reading, the last will and testament of Minerva Atreus. In it, Minerva had written her final earthly wishes,

The House bequeathing the house to her next of kin and all of its belongings, she put aside a solid sum providing her beloved caretakers Nester and Agatha with all they would need for the rest of their lives, along with a sealed letter reading: "Instructions for the Keeper of the House" to be given to whomever took legal ownership of it.

None of her next of kin came forward to claim the house. Some neighbors speculated that the relatives passed on such a beautiful home because of the rumored hauntings attached to it; the wild sobs of a young woman heard through the whirling winter winds as the year closed, coupled by a sturdy knocking that emanated onto the street even over Minerva's nightly piano playing. No neighbors or caretakers of the house ever asked Minerva about the sounds heard. They knew Minerva's teenage daughter had died there during childbirth along with her offspring.

They were a superstitious and God-fearing people, they understood it was best not to question the difficulties within families. They knew these things do not necessarily end with the closing of one's life. Sadly and strangely Minerva's daughter died on the very last night of the year, just as Minerva would years later. And so the house sat and sat for many many years, with only brief visits from the caretakers Nester and Agatha to air the house out and clip the lawn.

One day a distant relative of Rebecca's passed her information to the firm who handled Minerva's estate. They confirmed Rebecca as being next in the family line to inherit the house and all its belongings if she so wanted. Rebecca and her husband were thrilled and received the house gratefully.

They had heard of the odd happenings surrounding the house and its original residents; Rebecca and her husband thought how sad and exaggerated it was that Minerva's closest relatives couldn't or wouldn't receive this beautiful home. They themselves were glad, for this stroke of luck came at just the right time in their lives as they were starting a family together. And so, Rebecca requested an address for her distant relative in order to thank him or her properly. The request was denied, only a message was sent to Rebecca through the firm;

"Enjoy the house, please follow the clear instructions for the keeper of the house, and once you have gone simply pass this on."

With the arrival of Autumn, Rebecca and her husband moved into the house welcoming this new chapter of their lives; in this neighborhood, on this street, and in this house. It was the house of their dreams. And as the last of the season's leaves blew out, in came the arrival of their first child, their daughter was born.

And as their good luck would have it, Miss Eleanor, the daughter of the late caretakers Nester and Agatha, was quite a good and helpful hand to nanny their newborn baby. They were indeed happy and quite proud as they lived together in the house in the middle of the street.

# The Very Last Day and Night of the Year

Winter came and brought this warm and tidy family to the very last day and night of the year. On the eve of that new year, Rebecca baked a "special" bread for their evening dinner to celebrate their good fortune. As Rebecca opened her kitchen window the sweet smell of the baking bread twirled out into the clear cold air. Outside winter's wind whirled and whirled sweeping into the kitchen through the window with a sound like a long-reaching cry. Rebecca, a bit chilled, wrapped her sweater around her, laying her eyes out onto the horizon.

Rebecca's husband came into the kitchen,

"Rebecca, you'll freeze us out my love, it'll be the death of us."

"Oh my, of course, my darling, you are right indeed…I drifted off to another place, the sounds of winter have put a spell on me," said Rebecca.

Rebecca's husband immediately went to shut the window. As he closed it a last thick breeze charged in knocking down a row of books on the kitchen shelf. A letter with a golden wax seal embossed with the initials MA fell from the shelf of books, flat down onto the kitchen counter.

It read "Instructions for the Keeper of the House."

Her husband looked at her calmly,

"The windows stay shut for now Rebecca, the baby will catch a chill."

He picked up the books that had fallen and set them back, handing the letter to his wife.

"Oh," Rebecca said, "the letter, I was wondering where it went, I'll open it up a bit later on."

Rebecca flipped through the pages of one of the books titled "The Ancient Art of Bird Watching," that had fallen off the shelf. It was quite an aged and well-used book with its hard edges now soft and fraying and its pages delicate and smooth.

It contained the most beautiful and detailed gouache illustrations of birds known to roam the earth as well as those of mythological and mystical origins. She stopped at a gorgeous illustration of the three winged monsters Homer named Harpies from one of the scenes in *The Odyssey*, as they seized the huddled daughters of Pandarus. Rebecca's husband looked over her shoulder onto the illustration. They looked at the image together. "Excuse me, sir" said a gentle voice from outside the kitchen door.

Both Rebecca and her husband looked up at Eleanor standing in the archway of the kitchen door with their newborn swaddled sweetly in her arms. Eleanor's warm brown eyes shined as the sun streamed onto them through the window.

"Might I shut the opened windows in the house, the winds are picking up?"

"Yes, of course, Eleanor, you've read our minds," said Rebecca. Eleanor nodded with a smile. She looked at Rebecca and her husband and said,

"Ahhh I see you've found Minerva's prized book."

"Oh my, was it a favorite of hers?" asked Rebecca.

"It's quite beautiful and delicate. We should rebind it."

ANASSA
JAPAN
THE HOUSE IN
COOKING 101
JOYCE
HOMER

Rebecca touched the page and felt how thin it was.

"Yes," confirmed Eleanor, "it was very special to her. She read it and reread it, again and again, particularly this time of year. I imagine she was most interested in the birds of winter."

Eleanor watched as Rebecca slipped the golden sealed letter back in the page for safekeeping, shut it, and set the fine book in its rightful place.

"Eleanor, sweetheart. It's New Year's Eve. I'm certain you have lovely plans for the evening, please take the rest of the day off. I'll take the baby and you get going. Have some fun," said Rebecca. "Happy New Year, Eleanor!"

"Yes, Happy New Year," said Rebecca's husband.

"Well thank you!" said Eleanor.

She gave the baby a cuddle and placed her in her mother's arms. "A blessed and safe New Year to you all," said Eleanor as she left the family to enjoy the evening amongst themselves.

# New Year's Day

The kitchen quickly filled with a warmth and the sweet smell of fresh bread baking once again. Rebecca's husband pulled his wife close to him and wrapped his arms around her and their newborn child, kissing Rebecca gently. They looked into each other's eyes not needing to say a word. They were happy and they were proud.

By early evening, Rebecca heard a sturdy knocking at their front door. She peeked out the windows on either side of the door and saw two children standing there, a boy and a girl, both dressed formally, though their clothes were somewhat wrinkled and a bit soiled. She imagined it was from a day of play.

The boy was dressed in a long dark grey pant, a light grey button-up dress shirt with a white ribbon tied around his neck like a simple bow tie. He wore suspenders and a grey suit jacket. He stood in worn buckled shoes that needed a good polish.

The girl wore a beige prairie dress with brown lace-up boots and a deep-colored wool church coat. Her long brown hair parted in the middle and tied in pigtails gathered with white ribbon at each end that fell well below her shoulders. They looked quite rumpled for children of this neighborhood.

They saw Rebecca looking at them through the glass pane. The young girl, looking about eleven years old, smiled and waved. Rebecca waved back and opened the door to greet them.

# A Boy & A Girl

"Well hello there," said Rebecca.

"Hello. How do you do?" said the girl.

"Just fine, thank you," said Rebecca. "Who may I say I have the pleasure of meeting?"

The girl said, "I am Happy, and this is my younger brother, Virgil."

"Hello, Happy." Rebecca extended her arm to the young girl. They shook hands and smiled gently at each other. Rebecca turned and looked squarely at Virgil. "Hello young sir," declared Rebecca.

She reached her hand out to him. Virgil kept his hands by his side.

"Oh, I'm sorry. Is something the matter?" said Rebecca.

Happy said, "Not at all Mrs…" she waited.

"Mrs. Boread, my dear," said Rebecca.

"My brother is quite shy, Mrs. Boread," said Happy, "and doesn't speak often. He means well enough."

"I understand," said Rebecca.

Rebecca looked at Virgil, "That is just fine. How may I help you this evening?"

Happy said, "We were skipping by and we smelled your lovely bread baking. We are heading home but still have a ways to go…we thought maybe we could have some!"

Virgil tugged on Happy's arm sleeve. Happy turned to him and patted his head.

"He's quite hungry Mrs. Boread," said Happy.

Just then, Mr. Boread came into the entryway holding his newborn daughter. He cuddled her close as he stood beside the family portrait of Great Great Aunt Minerva, sitting at a grand piano, the same piano that still lived in the house. Minerva's hands gently laid on the piano keys, behind her, on the window sill, sat a row of simple glass jars with shiny golden lids sealed on top. The newborn was lovingly wrapped in a soft white blanket, only her eyes and the tip of her nose peeked out. The newborn made a sweet little cooing sound. Virgil tugged on Happy's arm sleeve. Happy patted him once again. Happy and Virgil looked at the little one and returned a hearty cooing sound straight back to the baby girl, though instead of sweet baby coos they sounded more like squawks of a bird. Of course, these sounds made the baby cry. Mr. Boread looked into the wide faces of young Happy and Virgil standing at his door. He looked at their worn shoes and dirt-smudged faces, he noticed their hands were quite slender and their nails unkempt and a bit too long.

He hushed his baby with warm cuddles.

"Rebecca?" said Mr. Boread.

Rebecca looked at her husband, she could see concern in his eyes. She glanced at the children at their door. Her heart dropped for a moment, she quickly brushed her hair back in a swing and announced, "My darling, we have two young visitors this afternoon, please welcome them."

Happy leaned forward towards Mr. Boread,

"We'd like some fresh bread. The aroma was drifting down the street and it lead us right here. May we come in Sir?"

"These little ones have the scent of vultures," Rebecca laughed. "Indeed she is certain what she wants. Come in children, come in and please follow me."

Mr. Boread felt oddly unfriendly towards the children, he nodded to his wife, addressed the children with a slow, "…yes…welcome." Happy looked up into Mr. Boread's eyes and said, "Thank you for inviting us in."

Happy took her brother's hand and dragged him forward, Virgil's shoulder caught on the bottom-edged frame of Minerva's portrait, tripping both Virgil and Happy off balance. They both let out a scared sound similar to their earlier squawk. Mr. Boread watched as Happy and Virgil followed Rebecca into their kitchen. He quietly trailed behind them, stopping at the portrait to straighten out its frame. He stood just outside the kitchen door looking in as Rebecca sat the hungry children at their kitchen table. Both children tucked themselves tightly against the table and ceremoniously rubbed their hands against the wooden table top making humming noises that rhythmically moved their chins down and up, up and down, their lips pressed shut with a precise slim smile drawn on their faces.

Rebecca looked at them with curiosity and listened for a moment to the whirling sound they were making, like sounds of cooing pigeons gathered on a sill.

She laid one of her two freshly baked bread loaves onto her marble counter by the window. The last bits of the setting sun gently landed onto the bread illuminating it with a very pretty rose tone. As Rebecca cut into the loaf, a single stream of sunlight shot through one of the many simple glass jars that were lined up on the window sill, the very same glass jars that were captured in the old family oil painting of Minerva that remained in the entryway of this house.

As Happy looked up at the bread, the sunbeam shot through the jar and struck into her eye, she didn't blink. She saw the many jars resting on the window sill.

"Ahhh, Mrs. Boread, those jars, those jars, they have stolen the sunlight," said Happy.

Mrs. Boread reassured Happy that the sunlight indeed was not captured in the jars, it simply shines through them at this time of day. Happy insisted that the light was locked in the jars and Rebecca needed to let them out,

"It just isn't fair Mrs. Boread to capture the light, it just isn't fair," she continued.

"My dear, my dear, please, settle down," said Rebecca.

Rebecca placed one slice of the fresh bread on each of the two pretty little green plates.

"One for Happy, one for Virgil," Rebecca said, as she placed each plate, in front of each child.

Happy and Virgil together looked up at Rebecca, the aroma of delicious fresh bread infused the room, they pushed their plates away and in unison demanded,

"Let the sunlight out, let it out!" Mr. Boread anxiously watched from the doorway. He held himself still not wanting to cross his wife's hospitality. Rebecca stood quietly confused looking at the children and their full plates of bread. "Children, aren't you hungry?" asked Rebecca.

Slowly and very gently, Virgil opened his mouth and said in an odd squawk

"Yes, yes we are, please open them Rebecca and let out the sun." Rebecca was surprised to hear Virgil speak and to say her first name. Did she tell them her name or did her husband say her name for them to hear by the front door? Either way, it was quite inappropriate.

Rebecca pushed the plates back towards the children and said,

"Please have your bread dear ones and I will let the sun out."

As Mr. Boread watched, Rebecca turned to the window sill, picked up the first simple glass jar sitting in the row of jars, and unscrewed the sealed golden lid of one simple glass jar.

...a silence came over the room, a beautiful calm filled it.

The children softened their posture and let out a long and gentle coooo.

They looked at Rebecca with heart-filled eyes and gently tipped their heads side by side with smiles that grew and grew and grew. Their teeth darkened and pressed out from their now wide opened mouths lengthening into beaks that slowly began to snap snap SNAP until they were sturdy and formed.

The sound of popping arose around them as the buckles on Virgil's shoes opened like the mouth of a flower blooming, large claws reached out pushing the shoes back like the curling of burning paper. The thread in their coat buttons unraveled allowing their brown feathered chests to finally rise in breaths out and in, their long fingers and unkempt nails shimmered into shiny black talons.

The braids on Happy's head lifted and waggled into brown beaded wings, creating a whirl of wind that swept across the room in a figure eight. As the creatures erupted out of their previous molds they rose up more and more into themselves, disrupting the tidy kitchen with a cacophony of bleats, clutching and scratching from their newborn hooks, flapping their wide wings and screaming in squawks.

Rebecca's husband called to his wife,

"Rebecca, Rebecca come to me."

Rebecca was still, staring at the creatures, entranced by them, not responding to her husband. The Boread's newborn daughter suddenly began to wail. Rebecca continued to be mesmerized by the creatures, no response towards her daughter's cries. The creatures turned their still human heads and big blinking eyes towards the newborn's sounds. As they raised their feathered chests up and then down, they let out a piercing squawk in unison.

The baby immediately went quiet. Mr. Boread held his child in his arms closely and stood absolutely still, his eyes keenly on the creatures. The creatures locked claws, hand in hand, arched their feet like a ballerina pointing her toes, landing her feet and gliding forward, savoring each moment, stretching and sliding step by step towards Mr. Boread who held his small daughter tightly in his arms, swaddled in her delicate white blanket. Mr. Boread stood still keeping sharp eye contact with the creatures as they neared.

The creatures reached Mr. Boread and the baby.

They stood face to face with him.

They were silent.

Mr. Boread was silent. The newborn was silent, save the rising and falling of their breaths, creating a gentle whirling wind that moved around the room in figure eights. Rebecca stood up calmly and walked over to the creatures, her husband, and her newborn. Rebecca turned to her husband and said,

"They are so hungry, we shall invite them for New Year's Eve dinner, my darling."

"Rebecca, look at them, look at who they are!" said Mr. Boread. Rebecca and her husband looked at them, with their pale hungry faces, and long-grown claws, their big sweet eyes that called you into their sturdy dark beaks.

As they looked at them their large beaded wings began to spread open and lengthen, their claws kneading into the wood floor and their beaks opened wide releasing a long thin shrill.

Mr. Boread pulled his wife to him as he held their newborn daughter firmly into his chest. Rebecca quietly turned away from her faithfully devoted husband and their newborn darling. She reached out to Happy, or what was Happy, looked into her eyes and slowly lifted her hand and gently pet her brown beaded wing. Happy bowed her head and let out a cooooooo.

Virgil stepped away from Happy and swift like lightning snatched the newborn from Mr. Boread's arms. The baby wailed. Mr. Boread leapt towards Virgil as Virgil let out a strong wind-filled squawk that simply threw Mr. Boread on his back.

His body lay still.

No movement.

No sound.

Rebecca looked at them all, seemingly without much feeling, she turned back and returned to her place by the kitchen counter, slicing pieces of bread and piling them up on the pretty little green plates for Happy and Virgil. Happy and Virgil squawked stretching and stepping back over to the table, their little green plates piled with slices of fresh bread. Virgil kept the baby tucked under his wing and muffled her sounds. They leant over and feasted on the bread. They squawked once their plates were cleared. Rebecca placed more slices of bread onto the little green plates. They feasted, they squawked…so on and so on, as the bread finished, Rebecca continued to cook and serve, and on and on, until night fell. As the clock struck midnight, ringing in the New Year, the creatures returned back to their previous appearance, as a girl and a boy. Happy quietly picked up the white cloth napkin from the table and wiped each corner of her mouth, she turned to Virgil and did the same for him.

"Hmmmmm," said Virgil.

"Quiet!" said Happy sharply.

"Ohhh I'm so glad he liked it," said Rebecca.

Virgil clapped. Happy crushed Virgil's hands into hers "I said QUIET you fat little boy."

Happy stood up from the kitchen table, straightened out her dress, and walked softly over to Rebecca.

Rebecca stood, calmly and looked at her, "Yes dear, what is it that you want?"

Happy lifted up onto her tiptoes, pushed back Rebecca's beautiful ravened curls behind her ear, and whispered to her. Happy landed back onto the soles of her laced-up brown leather boots, still looking at Rebecca. Rebecca looked at Happy and said clearly,

"Yes, I promise."

Happy walked back to Virgil who sat at the kitchen table, he stood up at attention.

Happy took hold of Virgil's hand, and they began to walk out of the kitchen. Happy turned her head towards Rebecca and said, "This was lovely Rebecca, we will be back for more."

Rebecca watched, in stillness as they stepped over Mr. Boread's body, walking out the kitchen door. Happy's arm reached back lengthening towards Mr. Boread's body, her fingers stretched out into shiny black talons, they took hold of his scalp, dragging him with them as they continued towards the door.

Virgil opened the door for Happy and her newest prey. As they walked down the grey stone path into the darkness, their bodies opened swiftly into brown beaded wings flapping and they lifted into the night's sky.

Rebecca heard herself scream out, her baby daughter began to wail, she swung her head left to right, right to left searching for her, she did not know where her baby's cries were coming from.The room began to turn, as Rebecca's horror rose her body descended down onto the floor, she cradled herself,

"My Lord, my good Lord, what have I done, please please help us..."

An old woman appeared standing over Rebecca, she held a simple glass jar in her hand. Her lips moved in whispers. She unscrewed the shiny golden lid from the jar and began whirling it over Rebecca and her cries. She moved the jar swiftly and gently in a figure eight, one after the other, after the other. With each figure eight she gathered the swells of pain that filled the air around Rebecca.

Rebecca's eyes followed the movements and, as she looked into the face of the old woman, she recognized her from the old family portrait that hung in the

entryway, The portrait of her Great Great Aunt Minerva, sitting at the piano, the same piano that still lived in the house, with Minerva's hands gently laid on the keys of the piano.

Behind her on the window sill sat a row of simple glass jars, just like the one she was swirling over Rebecca right now. Just like the one Rebecca unsealed in the kitchen earlier that evening. Rebecca fell to sleep.

Time passed and entered into the early hours of the New Year's Day, Rebecca awoke in her bedroom, to her baby's cries. She felt numb.

What she recalled of the previous evening could not have been real and she decided it was simply a terrible dream. As Rebecca glanced over to the baby's bassinet, there she lay on her back, eyes wide open, hands and her legs moving strongly, her mouth open and shrilling. She heard the soft cry of a woman surrounding her, piano playing rose up from the living room. She was so very tired and thought to fight against it, lift her baby up and soothe her back to sleep, go downstairs and see what and who was there, but she just could not. Instead, she surrendered to the deep winter slumber that enveloped her and returned to the comfort of her warm bed and slept,

and slept,

and slept.

# Rebecca & Her Children

After that night, Rebecca was no longer the same. Her days and nights and nights and days passed into each other. She became reclusive and rarely left the house. She spoke to no one other than Eleanor, the caretakers' daughter, who had become a steady fixture to the household, arriving most mornings and leaving just before nightfall. Rebecca never mentioned her faithful and devoted husband to Eleanor. Eleanor knew her place and stayed on the task of caring for Rebecca's growing young daughter. In the beginning, Eleanor did ask when Mr. Boread would return and when he had left.

Rebecca would always answer in the same way, "No relenting for any of us, Eleanor" and simply changed the subject.

The neighbors would come to call on Rebecca and her beautiful family for a while with no answer. As winter softened into spring, stories took hold of why Rebecca and her lovely family were never seen or heard of outside of the rise of piano playing coming from the house some early mornings and very late nights.

As December arrived once again to the house in the middle of the street, passing the one-year birthday of Rebecca's daughter and approaching that fateful New Year's Eve night when the creatures had arrived and taken hold of Rebecca and her family, Rebecca began repeating over and over to Eleanor that they must be prepared for the children when they arrive again.

"We must make it lovely and fine for them. They get so hungry and need so much. Those sweet lonely children. I wonder," Rebecca would say, "if they have a family at all."

Eleanor listened and listened as Christmas day passed and New Year's Eve approached. She had grown up hearing a cautionary tale told to her by her late parents, Nester and Agatha, to be aware of two wicked bird-like creatures, disguised as children who might come to this house in the middle of the street just before nightfall on New Year's Eve and knock and knock asking to be invited in and feed because they were very very hungry. Her parents told her, never never let them in.

Eleanor had been frightened of this story as a little girl but when she got a bit older she asked them, why did these creatures come to this house? Her parents told her, they are let loose on those that owe a debt, they smell their shame and fear and know they can feed off of it forever and ever until there is nothing left of them, and then they simply move on to find more. Once Eleanor was old enough she thought her parents superstitious with their odd and very silly tale. On the very last day of the whole year, Rebecca was in the kitchen perfecting her New Year's Eve bread and her delicious Christmas delights. Eleanor stood by the kitchen door watching her.

The vibrance Rebecca once had when they first met had faded, it was replaced with a desperate need to prepare perfectly for the return of the children that had been her guests the year before. Eleanor entered the kitchen and approached Rebecca. "How lovely, the smell of your fresh baking bread is, Mrs. Boread."

Rebecca didn't seem to hear and continued to read from the recipe book she held in her hands.

"It is a bit chilly in here, shall I shut the window?" said Eleanor.

Rebecca, looked up at her with loving eyes, "Yes, sweetheart. Please take care of this."

As Rebecca looked up at Eleanor, Eleanor caught a moment of sadness within Rebecca's eyes.

Eleanor said, "I'm so sorry Mr. Boread is not here Mrs. Boread." Rebecca looked at her, tears filled her eyes, she waited a moment, clasped her hands, lifted her head, and said, "No relenting for any of us, my dear."

A strong whirl of wind blew in, Eleanor immediately went to shut the window. As she closed it the last of a thick breeze charged in under the sill, knocking down the row of books on the kitchen shelf. Eleanor lent down and gathered the books, placing them back on the shelf.

She picked up the last fallen book, "The Ancient Art of Bird Watching." It opened up to a frayed and thinning page marked by the letter with the golden wax seal embossed with the initials MA, standing for Rebecca's Great Great Aunt, Minerva Atreus. Eleanor lifted the letter out of the book and turned it to its front, which read: "Instructions for the Keeper of the House." The letter had never been opened, the seal never broken.

"I believe this is your letter. Yours to open, Mrs. Boread," Eleanor read: "Instructions for the Keeper of the House," and handed Rebecca the letter. Eleanor placed *The Ancient Art of Bird Watching* on the kitchen counter. It was opened to a page with a remarkable gouache illustration titled *Homer: The Odyssey*. The Harpies seize the terrified daughters of Pandarus.

Eleanor looked at the watercolored illustrations. She saw clearly the wicked bird-like creatures, with wide pale hungry faces and stretched-out claws, hovering over three huddled maidens. The soft sobs of a woman surrounded the room, the same sounds that are so often heard at the end of each year in this house.

Eleanor had always assumed they came from the way the walls and the winter wind settled against each other in the house…but now her heart sunk. She felt afraid inside. Rebecca calmly went to the window, opened it wide. The wind mixed in, fading whatever sounds were building in the kitchen. Rebecca handed the sealed golden letter to Eleanor and said,

"Please place this back in the book for me sweetheart, and pop it on the shelf."

Eleanor nodded and did what she was told, no questions asked. Rebecca went back to quietly reading her recipes. Eleanor suddenly interrupted Rebecca, "Excuse me, Mrs. Boread, I feel a bit unsettled and under the weather, might

I go home early today?" Before Rebecca could answer a sturdy knocking was heard at their front door.

Eleanor dropped into herself with panic.

Rebecca looked at her, "Eleanor, it's New year's Eve. Ahhh, I believe our children have arrived!"

Eleanor did not move. The knocking continued.

"Now dear, please answer the door and invite them in," stated Rebecca.

Eleanor told herself, *I am being quite ridiculous*. "Yes, of course, Mrs. Boread."

Eleanor walked to the front door, she peeked out the windows on either side of the door and saw two children standing there, a boy and a girl, both dressed formally, though their clothes were somewhat wrinkled and a bit soiled. The boy was dressed in a long dark grey pant, a light grey button-up dress shirt with a white ribbon tied around his neck like a simple bow tie. He wore suspenders and a grey suit jacket. He stood in worn buckled shoes that needed a good polish.

The girl wore a beige prairie dress with brown lace-up boots and a deep colored wool church coat. Her long brown hair parted in the middle and tied into pigtails, gathered with white ribbon at each end that fell well below her shoulders. They looked quite rumpled for children of this neighborhood. They saw Eleanor looking at them through the glass pane. The young girl, looking about eleven years old, smiled and waved.

Eleanor looked at their wide pale hungry faces, she looked at their unkempt dirtied nails…she saw the glint in the young girl's eyes and as the boy moved his arms straight against the sides of his body and his hands hung long against his pant pockets, shiny black talons stretched out from his narrow fingers as he slide them into his pockets. Eleanor now knew what her parents had said was the truth. Rebecca came up beside Eleanor walking slowly as she held the hand of her waddling one-year-old daughter.

"Please Eleanor, take her and I will attend to our guests." Eleanor felt numb but became automatic in her movements

and knelt down to reach for the little girl's hand. Rebecca's little daughter stepped towards her one foot at a time, trying to keep her balance until she fell into Eleanor's open arms.

Rebecca opened the door, "Welcome back children, welcome back."

# Ellie

After that night, the neighbors no longer spotted Eleanor arriving most mornings and leaving just before nightfall as she had done previously. Other nannies came and went over the years to mind Rebecca's growing daughter, it seemed none stayed long.

The neighbors continued to witness and report to the town keepers that on the very last day and night of the whole year they would without fail, see two young children, a boy, and a girl knocking at the front door of the house. These two children would knock and knock and knock, over and over again until the door would open to invite them in. On the seventh anniversary of Rebecca and her husband's move into the house, and the seventh year of Rebecca's daughter's life, no nanny was seen at all and the two children that visited on that New Year's Eve arrived but never left. The very hungry children stayed and lived in the house with Rebecca and her growing daughter.

The beautiful house changed into boxed-filled rooms buried in dust and clutter. The small wooden gate with the shiny black handle in the front of the house became difficult to open and its crisp white color dirtied.

The kitchen was littered with pots and pans and foul rotten food eating up the tiles on the floor, with egg shells brimming over dirty bowls and a breeding family of vermin settling into the warm wooden cabinets. Rebecca's young daughter appeased the hungry children, giving them first choice at meals,

17

eating what they discarded, and giving them what they wanted, as her mother had taught her to do. Her mother explained to her how important it was to take care of the very hungry children for they had so little and she had so much. She must share and please them, these poor children.

And once again, it came, the very last day and night of the whole year. Rebecca and her hungry children sat in the living room discussing what delights they would feast on that night, Rebecca's daughter watched them from the piano bench and listened. This would be the first year no nanny was present and it would be just them in the house. A draft blew into the living room. Rebecca's daughter stood up to follow it into the kitchen. As always, this time of year, Rebecca would open the windows quite wide in the kitchen to cast out the soft sobs that arrived as the year closed, along with the lingering of piano playing that always surrounded the house. Happy clocked the movements of Rebecca's young daughter. Happy glanced at Virgil. He looked back at her and nodded. The children were agitated. They were very very hungry and they wanted to be fed.

Rebecca's daughter tapped her mother's shoulder, but her mother did not respond.

Virgil opened his mouth wide, his beak formed quickly and it let out a shrill. Rebecca reached over and pet him, he quieted. Rebecca's daughter slipped away into the kitchen. The window was wide open, she went to shut it and as she did, a gust of wind came in and pushed down the books on the kitchen shelf. The book, *The Ancient Art of Bird Watching*, fell onto the floor at the young girl's feet. She picked it up as it opened to the page where the golden sealed letter lay.

JAPAN
THE HOUSE IN
COOKING 101
JOYCE
HOMER

She looked at the letter, it was shining so beautifully even though it was old and frayed, its golden seal sparkled. The front read: "Instructions for the Keeper of the House." The young girl looked at the opened page and its watercolored illustration that stared back at her with the three winged monsters Homer named Harpies from one of the scenes in *The Odyssey*, as they seized the huddled daughters of Pandarus. These were the mythological creatures with hungry pale faces, hosting bodies, half human, half bird known to snatch people from the earth and feed on them. Once they locate you and you let them in, they take hold of you like a plague. They are cursed with a deep hunger, their purpose is to relentlessly take more, forever emaciated, never satisfied. These monsters, she knew them, and here they were, in this book. Of course, here they were. All these years she told her mother again and again, can you not see, they are like vultures, in the night, as they feed.

Her mother would always say, "My dear, what you say about them is horrid. How could you, they need us and they love you. Why do you ruin everything? What a gift it is to give to them."

The young girl read and reread the book from front to back, all about the birds and their plans and how and why they feed and what they like to feed on, how they got here, and how and why they get to stay. She quietly and carefully took the book and the letter down to the basement where she could be alone. Though she felt shocked and full of rage, she also felt a deep relief that what she had felt, what she had known all these years was true WAS.

And what she had felt and knew was wrong, WAS.

And even, she knew she had to accept that her own mother, who she loved and admired, was in fact, wrong. That day, she saw her mother in a different light.

She saw her mother's shadows, her tragic flaws and she knew that no matter how much she wanted to believe her mother, she must not look away from the truth. She held the letter tight, closed her eyes for a moment, and said a prayer.

She opened her eyes, broke open the seal, and pulled out the letter. There was a list of instructions titled: "How to Keep the House Clean." Everything became clear to the young girl. She knew what she had to do. She tucked the letter safe inside her stockings. She went upstairs and saw their feast had begun.

The children were transforming and her mother asked her to sit with them. The young girl did not want to but her mother insisted, so she did. The clock struck eleven, it was the last hour of the very last night of the whole year. They squawked and squawked, demanding this year's jar be opened.

Rebecca satisfied their requests, as she had done each year for the last seven years since she had taken residence in the house in the middle of the street.

"Give us the light, Rebecca. Give it to us, now."

This light in the jar was not light at all. It was in fact a collection of all the sorrows, betrayals, and deceptions that occurred in Rebecca's family line: from Rebecca to Minerva back, back to their most ancient of ancestors.

The Harpies fed on this pain and were strengthened by it. Minerva had inherited the jars to keep safe and sound. But on the night Minerva's daughter gave birth, a single glass jar was unsealed by Minerva herself. That night Minerva wished to punish her daughter, once she found out the identity of the newborn's father. Minerva could not contain her rage and so instead of collecting the pain and suffering the year had brought, she unsealed it on the very last night of the year. It created a pocket of pain that The Harpies could smell. They were delighted for the opportunity to swoop down and snatch all they could get.

The young girl whispered to her mother, "Mother don't give it to them."

The mother said to her daughter, "Do not ruin everything. Do not. Can't you see what they need? I must take care of them. I promised and I am a woman of my word. They need us and they love you."

Happy and Virgil listening, squawked in agreement and clapped their claws. The young girl knew her mother could not see the truth anymore. She ran to the door. Virgil pulled her back, tucked her under his wing, and began to open his beak, and shrill, he dove his beak down into her. The winds blew banging on the outside window. The sound of a woman sobbing grew. The piano playing rose from the living room. Virgil missed his mark and lost hold of Rebecca's young daughter. She scrambled away from him. He clawed into her leg, slicing her skin open. Virgil and Happy went wild with excitement. Rebecca's daughter looked over at her mother, who was mindlessly cutting New Year's Eve bread as though the day and the night was a festive one.

She turned away from her mother.

She ran.

And she ran, out of the house and into the night.

As the story goes, there were great howling winds ripping through the trees from a wicked storm that ran through the neighborhood that night. The very next day when the town keepers went around to check on each of the residents, they went to the house in the middle of the street, the gate marked with tarnished black metal numbers that read seventeen. They pushed and pushed the now dirtied white gate that led them down the grey stone path to the front door.

They knocked and knocked with no answer.

They found their way in. No one was found in the house and Rebecca was never seen again. One brave neighbor did report to the town keepers that on that night, he saw two creatures that flew up into the night sky holding a woman in their grip as they rose up. How very sad it was for Rebecca and her faithful and devoted husband, who had lived in the house in the middle of the street. They were so happy and they were so proud.

Many years passed, the neighborhood changed and the stories of Rebecca and her family, Minerva and her daughter faded away as most old stories do.

And the house sat and sat and sat,
empty and quiet,
never a visitor,
never a sound.
Until today.

# Instructions for the Keeper of the House

My name is Ellie, or it was then when I lived in the house in the middle of the street. After a lifetime away, I have returned. I am old now. Rebecca was my mother and her faithful and devoted husband was my father. After Eleanor, many nannies came and went. They all met the same fate as my father, as Eleanor, and even as my mother did, at the hands of the very hungry creatures. I could not seem to get away from the family's debt. No matter how far I traveled, it remains open and it remains mine to do. I have finally accepted this. I expect the creatures to sense that I have returned and they will, no doubt, show up on the very last day and night of the year. And I will be waiting for them. I know now that my mother was not a careful woman. She had heard the old stories, she had been warned by the elders, yet she dismissed it and made her own rules. There are consequences for that. My mother accepted the house without following through with the one requirement passed to her,

"Enjoy the house, please follow the clear instruction for the keeper of the house, and once you have gone simply pass this on." And she will now join the collection of sobs that rain down in this house, trying to warn us when the Harpies arrive. I know if I don't stop them they will wait for the opportunity to feed on my children and my children's children and so on and so forth until the debt is closed and the truth is remembered. Night is falling now on this last night of the year. I sit in the armchair Minerva died in. Minerva's black wooden chest rests beside me filled with all the golden sealed jars, I will follow her instructions to keep this house clean.

I wait. I wait.

Nothing.

The clock strikes nine.

No one.

I wait.

My mind drifts to fond thoughts of my mother, my regrets build. I remember turning away from her that last night when I left as a young girl. She was humming and cutting her fresh baked bread. I turned away from her and ran away forever.

The clock strikes ten.

I hear them, the sturdy knocking at my front door. My heart does not sink. I am no longer afraid.

I am happy they have come.

I approach the entryway to the front door of what is now my house. I look up at the portrait of my mother's Great-Great Aunt Minerva. I peek out of the windows on either side of the door and I see two children standing there, a boy and a girl, both dressed formally, though their clothes are somewhat wrinkled and a bit soiled.

The boy, Virgil dressed in a long dark grey pant, and a light grey button-up dress shirt with a white ribbon tied around his neck like a simple bow tie. He wears suspenders and a grey suit jacket.

He stands in worn buckled shoes that need a good polish.

The girl, Happy, wears a beige prairie dress with brown lace-up boots and a deep colored wool church coat. Her long brown hair parted in the middle and tied into pigtails, gathered with white ribbon at each end that fall well below her shoulders.

I open the door.

Happy steps up and looks right at me and smiles, "Well, hello there, Ellie. Happy happy New Year! Can we come in, please? We're so very hungry and you owe us so very much, after all we have done for you and your mother."

A foul smell exits from her mouth as she speaks to me.

Happy looks to Virgil.

Virgil steps up.

He cackles and opens his mouth wide, his teeth darken and press out lengthening into his sturdy formed beak that slowly begins to snap snap SNAP.

I walk away from the creatures.

I carry the black chest to the front of the door for them to see. Their eyes swell with eagerness taking in the many sealed jars. "Ahhh, I said, do you like my jars?"

"Open my jars, Ellie!" Happy squawked.

"They belong to us, your mother promised we could have them."

"Oh I see, you can't open them yourself, Happy?"

Happy's braids lifted and flapped into her beaded brown wings creating a whirl of wind. I sat and watched her. I had seen this so many times before.

The clock struck eleven.

"Give us the light, give us the light," they squawked, now fully transformed into themselves, hovering over me with their claws dangling. I get on my knees, and one by one I begin to open each jar, one after the other, after the other, letting out everything that had been held in them from as far back as the house of Atreus went.

Wild bellows lifted out of the jars, imprinting on the air, catching on the edges of the room saturating a silent fear into us.

"Do you want more?" I asked Happy and Virgil. They clamored with pleasure and squawked for more. I unsealed all the jars and let what was held, out. Images formed and floated through the air of unsightly evils and quiet betrayals.

The creatures clawed and rolled into each image, intoxicating themselves. I sat still on the floor under the portrait of Minerva. All the jars were unsealed and discarded on the floor of the foyer.

# The End

I had never seen the creatures so animated, so full of life soaring up and down, flapping and snapping so deliriously.

The elation they had from ingesting the pain and suffering of others was remarkable and terrifying.

I sat quiet.

I was not afraid for myself or my life.

I knew I was doing what I was meant to do.

I was satisfied and strong in my purpose, to end this.

I had faith in Minerva's instructions. It all had to be unsealed. As the generations filled the room certain feelings draped over me and spoke to me, trying to distort my thoughts.

I was prepared.

Minerva instructed me, I knew some of the images and reflections were truths and some were lies. I looked at each one carefully as they danced in front of me.

I felt them. I became aware of them and I faced them. Struggle to concentrate, this is one of the instructions Minerva gave.

Listen to learn—I did.

More will be revealed—It was.

The images seemed to fade. The creatures were now settled at the front door licking themselves like cats after a meal. The room was quiet.

Light smoke rose up from one of the jars, it settled down in front of me. It formed the image of my mother and my father in the kitchen, looking into each other eyes, happy and proud. And then, I saw the creatures feeding at the kitchen table.

My father was holding me and Virgil snatched me from him and tucked me under his wing. My father leapt towards Virgil to try to reach me. Virgil let out a mighty shrill and my father fell to the floor. He never got up again. The fury in my body shook me up to standing. I felt unsteady inside. I walked over to the creatures, face to face.

"Get out of my house."

They flapped and spat at me.

Happy squawked, "You invited us in and we are not done, not nearly."

"No creature, I did not invite you in. I have never invited you into my house.

Leave. Now."

I was clear and so they had no choice but to be clear as well. They couldn't smell the scent of shameful broken promises and past regrets harbored.

The space had nothing and no one willing to be taken. They knew that.

They wasted no time.

They moved on, indeed to find a sorry soul ripe for the taking. The clock struck twelve.

The New Year arrived.

As they walked out of the front door and into the night, their squawks shrilled as they lifted up flapping their brown beaded wings, waggling their pale hungry faces from side to side scanning for somewhere on earth where they could get more.

The moral of this tale lies here,
beware of the creature of more.
And lastly, be selective who you invite in.

# About the Author

Jennifer Sklias-Gahan grew up in New York raised by her single mother Stella and her extended Greek family. Like so many others then and now who arrived through Ellis Island, their wish was to escape poverty and to achieve the American dream.

There were no books in their house with the exception of a Greek cookbook and a few encyclopedias, so her grandmother would tell her stories, from Greek Myths, to memories about their own lives and the folklore of her ancestors. Jennifer was enchanted by these stories she listened to and wanted more. Her mother suggested she take her recess time and go to the school library, so she did. She steeped herself in the books she found. One day her librarian asked her what her favorite book was. She answered, *The Fairy Tales of Hans Christian Anderson*, in particular 'The Little Match Girl.'" Jennifer's librarian asked her to memorize the tale and tell it to the younger grades. She accepted.

Once she sat with the other younger children circled around her to listen and tell the tale—everything felt right, she knew clearly, storytelling was where she wanted to be and what she wanted to do. It was simply a magical way of finding yourself,finding others and seeing all the ways life can be lived.

This passion for both written and spoken storytelling has stayed with her as a writer, actor and producer as well as the founder of Demivoula Studios, and co-founder of 18 Bleecker Films. Jennifer still lives in New York with her husband, and has two children James and Stella Rose.